Della and Lila

Meet the

Monongahela Mermaid

As told by
Della Mitchell

Arranged by
Brianne Mitchell

Illustrated by

Sian Bowman

Mitchell Publishing
P.O. Box 1000
Brownsville, PA 15417

As told by Della Mitchell
Arranged by Brianne Mitchell
Illustrated by Sian Bowman

1st Edition
Mitchell Publishing
www.dellaandlila.com

ISBN: 9780986216107

To my best friend, Lila, thank you for being my sister.
And, to all of my family and friends,
thanks for being mine!
Love, Della

For Mitch, who makes all of our dreams come true.
Always and in all ways, Brianne

Thank you, to my husband and best friend Tim,
who has helped to make my passion my work.
Love always, Sian

* Ohio River

* Allegheny River

PITTSBURGH

PENNSYLVANIA
Pittsburgh

Wildlife of Pennsylvania
Can you find each of our
animal friends in this book? ✓

BALD EAGLE   GREAT HORNED OWL

WATERFOWL   FISH

TURTLE

BEAVER   OTTER

CHIPMUNK   RACCOON

FOX   WHITE-TAILED DEER

GRAY SQUIRREL

CLAIRTON

ELIZABETH

NEW EAGLE
MONONGAHELA

DONORA

MONESSEN
BELLE VERNON
FAYETTE CITY

CHARLEROI
ALLENPORT
STOCKDALE
ROSCOE
COAL CENTER   ELCO
CALIFORNIA

40

NEWELL

HILLER

West Brownsville

Mon River Basin

BROWNSVILLE

FREDERICKTOWN

40

UNIONTOWN

HOPWOOD

PENNSYLVANIA   FARMINGTON

N

Nemacolin Woodlands

STATE LINE

* Cheat River

FAIRMONT

WEST VIRGINIA

* West Fork River

* Tygart River

The Monongahela River

The Monongahela River

The Monongahela River begins in Fairmont, West Virginia, by the confluence of the West Fork and the Tygart Valley Rivers.

The Monongahela flows north, winding its way through Pennsylvania to "the Point", in Pittsburgh, where it meets the Allegheny River. Together, the Monongahela and Allegheny Rivers form the Ohio River.

The Monongahela River is approximately 128 miles in length.

The word "Monongahela" is of Native American origin and means "falling banks."

Coal and coke from western Pennsylvania have remained major industries along the banks of the Monongahela for many generations. Barges and trains carry countless tons of coal along the river each day.

TOP SECRET FACT: In addition to the familiar animals and fish who make the Monongahela River their home, there are also mermaids, monsters* and pirates who call the river their home too...
Shhhh...It will be our secret!

*The "monsters" aren't mean...just misunderstood. They are actually very helpful!

Hi, my name is Della and my little sister's name is Lila.

Our Lovey (that's another word for "grandmother") and our John (that's another word for "grandfather whose name is John") live right on the banks of the Monongahela River.

I spend a lot of time at their house – swimming, boating, fishing, collecting treasures and watching the water. I know our river really well.

Some might even say I am a Monongahela River expert. I have been a river expert for 5 years (because that's how old I am).

Being an expert means that you really know a lot about something.

One day, when my sister was following me around (like she always does), I saw a splash in the water. At first, I thought it was a duck because there are many species of ducks in the river. Some of my favorites are mallards, bufflehead and merganser ducks. There are also many species of geese, swan and other types of *waterfowl*. *But...* the splash I saw that day wasn't like anything I'd ever seen before.

It wasn't a bird or a fish or a duck (or any other type of waterfowl)...

...It was a...

MERMAID!

Waterfowl

is another word for a "bird that swims".

John teaches me all about our river's wildlife.

The mermaid had a light rainbow fin and was wearing a purplish-fuscia top. She had long brown hair with river grass braided through it. Her hair sparkled in the sunlight. She was wearing a lovely clamshell necklace decorated with shiny rocks, gems and coins. She had beautiful matching bracelets.

She was spectacular!

Spectacular is another way to say amazing.

I couldn't believe my eyes! A mermaid! Right in front of me! I didn't know what to do or say. But I didn't want her to leave; so I took a chance and said, as loudly as I could, "Hi! I'm Della! Um, where did you come from?" I hoped I wouldn't frighten her.

But to my absolute surprise, the mermaid waved and said hi back to me!

"Hi. I'm Marina, the Monongahela Mermaid. It's nice to meet you."

"It's nice to meet you too," I said slowly.

Marina looked troubled.

"Is everything alright?" I asked.

Marina looked around but didn't say anything. I felt like I should say something, anything, so she wouldn't swim away.

"I wish I could be a mermaid!" I said.

"Me too!" said Lila.

Marina looked at us and thought for a moment. "You know," she said, "it's very hard to be a mermaid."

"Why is it hard to be a mermaid?" I asked.

"Well," said Marina, "it's hard to be a mermaid because humans don't take care of our river. The river is my home. But I am sad to report that it's not doing well."

"I have traveled this river for many years.
I listen and watch and remember everything that happens
within its waters. I carry the stories, the secrets,
and the history of the river with me.
The Monongahela River is my home and it is in trouble.
I have journeyed to other rivers and they are in trouble too."

"Why are our rivers in trouble?" I asked quietly.

"Humans throw litter in the river. They throw away old tires, garbage, food and even cars! They put chemicals in the water that harm my fish and animal friends. My friends and I work hard to try and keep the water clean . But, we can't keep up. I just don't know what to do."

I could tell Marina was very sad.

"I know!" I said. "I know how to help! I will tell everyone not to litter in the river! I will explain to everyone that *pollution is very bad* and if we want to keep enjoying our river we have to keep it clean!"

"But, how will you do that?" Marina asked?

"I will make signs to hang around our town. I'll visit all of my neighbors and spread the news. I am even going to write a letter to the President! My sister, family and friends will all help! We are going to get started right away."

I took Lila's hand and ran off to find my mom.

My mommy was helping her mommy (my Lovey) plant flowers.

"Mommy! Mommy!
We have to help Marina! We have to save the river!"

My mom was a little confused, to say the least.
But, I explained everything as quickly as I could and
she understood in no time!

My mom said she would start making phone calls right away.

I asked her to call my friends Ally, Aidan, Claire, and Tessa (and their parents too, of course). My dad started calling our family from his phone. My grandparents, aunts, uncles and cousins would be on their way soon. I couldn't wait to get started.

The river needed our help!

It didn't take long for everyone to show up.

Now, we just needed a plan...

...and we came up with a GREAT one!

The grownups helped the kids create signs, posters and banners. The kids drew the pictures and the grownups helped with the words.

We used all *upcycled* materials to create our designs.

Upcycling means to reuse materials that would normally have been thrown away to make new, more beautiful items (like our posters)!

Don't Litter! Save the River!

With the help of our grownups,
we hung our *upcycled* posters all around town.

We put them in the coffee shop, post office, police station and even in the ice cream store (this was my favorite place to hang up posters).

We even set up an information booth at our town fair. All kinds of people came to visit our booth, learn more about our river and find out how they can help, too.

My friends and I worked very
hard all summer to educate everyone we
could about the Monongahela River.

Mr. President thanked us for our help.
He said he was very proud that we were
working so hard to save our river.

The President of the
United States of
America
even wrote a letter
back to me!

When I saw Marina again, she was so happy.
She couldn't believe all of the hard work my
friends and I had accomplished this summer.

And...Marina was excited to report
there was significantly
less pollution in the river than ever before.

The fish were happy,
the animals were happy,
the humans were happy..

...even all of the mermaids
were happy!

Della, Marina, Lila
Sisters, Mermaids, Friends

Marina swam over to the bank of the river.
She came as close as she could and reached out
to give my sister and I a big hug.

"Thank you Della and thank you Lila
for helping to save my home
and the home of so many others;
fish, animals, plants, and people," she said.

"People too?" I said.

"Yes, people too.
Even humans benefit from a clean, safe river."

I hugged Marina tight. She felt just like a human.

She was just like me!

As the sun was setting on the beautiful Monongahela River,
I stood with my family and waved goodbye to Marina.

I knew I would see her again someday soon.

It felt so great to help Marina and all of her friends .

I wonder who will need our help next?

CPSIA information can be obtained at www.ICGtesting.com
Printed in the USA
BVIW12n2059300315
393979BV00001B/1